SNAKE
HiS STORY

JAMES MARSHALL

HOUGHTON MIFFLIN COMPANY BOSTON

www.hmco.com/trade

Library of Congress Catalog Card Number: 00132437
ISBN 0-618-07320-5

Manufactured in the Singapore
TWP 10 9 8 7 6 5 4 3 2 1

FOR
FRANK AND
CAROLINE
MOURIS

When Snake was a baby he was very cute,
and his parents loved him a lot.

Very soon Snake was doing all the sneaky

things that snakes are so good at doing.

"Snake is such a tease," said all his friends.

Snake was also very good at hissing.
Of course, only a few silly butterflies
were frightened, but all the same he
had a magnificent hiss.
"He's going to be just like his father,"
thought Snake's mother.

But one day Snake began to behave in a very

strange manner. He had a faraway look in

his beady little eyes, he swayed back and forth,

and he seemed to be very happy.

His mother thought he was sick.

Doctor Wilson came over to examine Snake. When he had completed his examination, he took out a pen and paper and wrote a note to Snake's parents. "Now everyone knows that snakes cannot hear, but it seems that this little snake can hear. He's not sick; he's simply listening to music on the radio."

Snake's mother was concerned. "He won't be like the other little snakes," she thought. At Reptile Elementary the other little snakes gave Snake suspicious looks. They wrote notes behind his back. Snake felt uncomfortable about being different.

Snake was left out of all the schoolyard games.

One afternoon when Snake was coming home from school, he decided to stop off at the soda shop for a super strawberry shake.

At the next table, two mean-looking strangers were talking. When they saw Snake sitting there sipping his super strawberry shake, they stopped talking. "But we don't have to worry," said one of the gentlemen, "everyone knows that snakes can't hear."

So the two went right on talking, about robbing banks, about stealing purses from old walrus ladies, and about doing all sorts of mean things that nice people never would do. And Snake heard it all.

When the two left the soda shop, Snake followed at a distance and pretended to be minding his own business. But when they disappeared inside a bank, Snake took out a pen and paper and scribbled a note.

He gave the note to a nearby policeman.

Sure enough, when the strangers came out of the bank they were carrying money that didn't belong to them. "You're under arrest," said the policeman.

The robbers looked at Snake. "Maybe he can read lips," said one of them.

The next day at City Hall, Snake was given a medal and a transistor radio by the mayor himself. Snake's mother and father enjoyed the ceremony very much, even though they couldn't hear the mayor's long speech.

And Snake was very happy. He no longer worried about being different.

James Marshall, the creator of many hilarious books for children, including *Miss Nelson Is Missing* and *The Stupids Step Out,* has no rival when it comes to goofy fun. Filled with the same silly spirit and charm, his *Four Little Troubles* provide cozy comfort to young readers facing the universal troubles of childhood.

The *Four Little Troubles* series includes:

Eugene

Sing Out, Irene

Snake: His Story

Someone Is Talking about Hortense, written by Laurette Murdock